About the Author

Linda Uruburu is an author, lyricist and textile artist. She has been a professional musician, music publisher and song writer for most of her adult life. Her hobby and part time profession is designing patchwork.

About the Illustrator

Helen Schneider is an illustrator, an award winning international artist in the fields of recording, stage, and film (including a Diva for lifetime achievement), and a teacher of song interpretation. She has always had an interest in painting and drawing privately.

In 2008 they published their first children's books with Baumhaus Verlag. In 2019 their chapter book, *Lenny's Summertime Adventures*, was the first prize winner of the Literary Contest for the Center for Basque Studies.

The Colorful World of Frida Kato

Linda Uruburu
Illustrations by Helen Schneider

The Colorful World of Frida Kato

Nightingale Books

NIGHTINGALE PAPERBACK

© Copyright 2022
Linda Uruburu
Illustrations by Helen Schneider

A CIP catalogue record for this title is
available from the British Library.
ISBN 978-1-83875-498-3

Nightingale Books is an imprint of
Pegasus Elliot MacKenzie Publishers Ltd.
www.pegasuspublishers.com

First Published in 2022

Nightingale Books
Sheraton House Castle Park
Cambridge England

Printed & Bound in Great Britain

Acknowledgements

This book is inspired by the life and work of the artist Frida Kahlo.

It's moving day! The family just arrived at their new house. There is a very big moving van and lots of workmen and so many boxes.

"What can we do with the cat so she doesn't get lost?"

"Here's a room we can put her in while we empty the boxes."

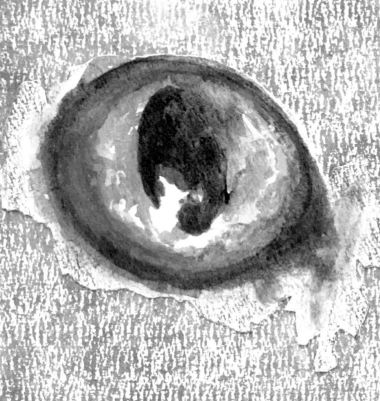

Poor Frida Kato!

A white cat locked in an empty white room. She looks in the mirror but all she can see are her eyes.

She's afraid. She's alone.

She wonders what happened to the world?

FRIDA KATO, TELL ME THIS,
IMAGINE THAT, IMAGINE THIS.
WHAT IS IT THAT YOU WANT TO SEE?
WHAT IS IT THAT WILL SET YOU FREE?

Wait, the workers left some paint!

She has an idea! She'll dip her long, soft white tail into the colors and paint pictures on the walls.

She'll paint what she would like to see. She'll paint what she knows. She'll paint her world, the world of Frida Kato!

FRIDA KATO, CAN YOU TELL
WHICH COLORS HERE WILL MAKE YOU WELL?
A SPLASH OF BLUE, A TOUCH OF GREEN,
YOU SEE THEM ALL INSIDE YOUR DREAM.

Frida finds red, yellow, and blue paint.

She picks blue for the color of her new house. She paints the house and then adds a field of yellow marigolds in her front yard and a few red poppies in the field. She notices on the floor the blue and yellow paint have dripped together and now she has green!

FRIDA KATO, TELL ME TRUE,
WHAT DO THE COLORS REALLY DO?
MIXED TOGETHER ON THE FLOOR
ASKING YOU TO PAINT SOME MORE!

Frida paints a green tree next to the house. But it looks lonely standing there all by itself. She tries mixing more colors. She dips her tail in each pot.

She adds a red fawn under the tree and a silly, black monkey in the leaves. And in the distance she paints the mountains and the beautiful blue sky.

She paints the beautiful yellow sun and a green parrot flying by.

FRIDA KATO, DO YOU SEE
YOU REALLY ARE A SILLY BEE.
YOU'RE NOT ALONE, YOU'RE IN A SEA
OF COLORS PAINTED ENDLESSLY.

Now the only thing missing is a friend.

So, Frida dips her tail in the red paint and mixes in a touch of white and then she paints a beautiful pink house for a very special friend to live in.

Now, Frida Kato looks in the mirror again. Suddenly, there she is! This time she sees herself, a beautiful white cat, in the middle of all her favorite colors.

She's not afraid anymore.

She is ready for her new world.

FRIDA KATO, NOW YOU SEE
THESE COLORS HERE WILL ALWAYS BE
A PART OF YOU, A PART OF ME,
A PICTURE FOR THE WORLD TO SEE.

"Okay, you can let the cat out now!"

The children run to the door and open it for the cat. Frida looks out the door and the first thing she sees is the most handsome black cat she has ever seen. "Frida," the kids whisper to her, "this is Diego Don Gato. He lives in the pink house next door."

Diego looks deep into Frida's eyes and they walk out of the house together into Frida's new world.

FRIDA KATO, SILLY CAT!
IMAGINE THIS, IMAGINE THAT.
WHAT WILL YOU THINK OF AFTER THAT?
FRIDA KATO, WHAT A CAT!

Lightning Source UK Ltd.
Milton Keynes UK
UKRC031929220922
409309UK00002B/4

* 9 7 8 1 8 3 8 7 5 4 9 8 3 *

Look Out Fish!

Written by Jenny Foster

Illustrated by Michael Evans

Look out, yellow fish.
The big fish is going
to eat you.

Snap!

Look out, blue fish.
The big fish is going
to eat you.

Snap!

Snap!

Look out, green fish.
The big fish is going
to eat you.

Snap!

Snap!

Look out, red fish.
The big fish is going
to eat you.

Snap!

Look out, big fish...

...the big, BIG fish is going to eat you!

12